# Kids lo
## *Choose Your (*

> "I like it because it is all about you."

Robert Nucci, age 9

> "I recommend these books because they make you read extraordinary things."

Daniel Hayes, age 8

> "These books make you feel like you are making the life-risking decisions, not reading about somebody making all of the choices as they write the book."

Matthew Fiaschetti, age 10

> "I like *Choose Your Own Adventure* because it feels like you're actually in the real book."

Alexander Rivera, age 9

> "I love these books because some are haunted and some are not. There are a bunch of adventures and there are a bunch of different endings. That is what I like about *Choose Your Own Adventure*."

Maddie Ryley, age 8

# CHOOSE YOUR OWN ADVENTURE®

## SURF MONKEYS

### BY JAY LEIBOLD

ILLUSTRATED BY GABHOR UTOMO
COVER ILLUSTRATED BY MARCO CANNELLA

CHOOSECO®
WAITSFIELD, VERMONT

*Surf Monkeys* © 1992 R. A. Montgomery
Warren, Vermont. All Rights Reserved.

Artwork, design, and revised text ©2017 Chooseco LLC,
Waitsfield, Vermont. All Rights Reserved.

Book design: Stacey Boyd, Big Eyedea Visual Design

For information regarding permission, write to:

**CHOOSECO**

P.O. Box 46, Waitsfield, Vermont 05673
www.cyoa.com

ISBN-10: 1-937133-24-9
ISBN-13: 978-1-937133-24-5

Published simultaneously in the United States and Canada

Printed in Canada

9 8 7 6 5 4 3 2 1

*The author would like to thank
Pat Reed—poet, surf aficionada,
and lifelong wave worshiper—without
whose help this book could not have
been written. Her knowledge and love
of the ocean provided much of the
inspiration for this book.*

# BEWARE and WARNING!

This book is different from other books.

You and YOU ALONE are in charge of what happens in this story.

There are dangers, choices, adventures, and consequences. YOU must use all of your numerous talents and much of your enormous intelligence. The wrong decision could end in disaster—even death. But don't despair. At any time, YOU can go back and make another choice, alter the path of your story, and change its result.

You are spending your summer vacation with your Uncle Dave in California. You are a natural in the water and quickly learn surfing just like Dave did when he was younger. Your friend Jorge, one of the gnarliest surfers you have ever met, disappears one day under mysterious circumstances. Recently, Jorge has become close with a tough gang of local surfers called the Surf Monkeys. Are they behind his disappearance? What do they know about the oil rig off the coast that they aren't telling you? And meanwhile, the geological clock is ticking down to the Big One, an earthquake that promises to shake up more than your investigation... Good luck!

You're the first surfer out. It's a perfect morning at the cove, and the ocean swells are smooth and glassy.

This is the best summer you've ever had, you muse as you paddle out on your board. Just think: you could have been stuck back home for the past two months, sweltering in the Indiana humidity, if you hadn't hatched a plan to spend your vacation with your Uncle Dave in California. But now here you are on a tranquil August morning on the central coast of California, looking forward to ripping your first wave of the day. The only thing is, it seems strange that there's no one else out yet.

You sit up on your board, still a little sleepy, and look around. You're about 200 yards out now, near the reef that creates the cove's breakwater. The rocky shore bluffs shimmer in the dawn light, and the lighthouse sits silently at the top of the cove. You wonder where your buddy Jorge is. Usually he's the first surfer out.

Then, out of the corner of your eye, you notice something floating in the kelp beds outside the reef. As you paddle over to it, you see that it's a loose surfboard lifting in the swells. Coming closer, you recognize the dark blue fiberglass covered with a collage of decals. It's your friend Jorge's board, and it's floating strangely in the water.

*Turn to the next page.*

You look around but see no sign of anyone. Raising the front of the board out of the water, you notice a chunk of its nose has been torn off— leaving the clean, sharp marks of a shark's teeth! Could Jorge have gone out earlier this morning and been attacked by a shark?

You look around. There are a few sea lions rolling lazily in the waves breaking offshore on the reef. If there had been a shark attack, the sea lions would have vanished. All seems peaceful. But your instinct tells you that something is horribly wrong.

The thought of losing your close friend makes you feel terribly sad and lonely. You think of your family back in Indiana. It's hard to believe summer is almost over. It seems like only yesterday you were feeling restless at home, walking through the new green corn.

School had just ended, and you could feel the long, hot summer stretching before you. That's when you started thinking about Uncle Dave. He lives here in California, where he is a software engineer, but his job is just a way to support his real passions of surfing and fishing. He visited your family at Christmas, and you were captivated by his tales of adventure on the wild Pacific. Before your uncle left, he invited you to spend your summer vacation with him.

*Turn to page 4.*

# 4

The thought of cool ocean breezes sounded pretty good, especially as the hot midwestern summer approached. Your mother intended to have you fix up the house over the summer. But with the help of a couple of phone calls from Dave, you finally convinced her to let you go.

You arrived in June in the small town where your uncle lives. It is foggier than you imagined, and a little sleepy, bordered by a lighthouse to the north and a harbor to the south. But as your uncle said, it has the most challenging surf on the coast. You were hardly unpacked before Dave raised his bushy eyebrows, waggled his salt-and-pepper goatee, and asked, "Ready to rip some gnarly waves?"

Dave threw two surfboards into his jeep, and you headed down to Surfer's Cove, as it's known to tourists. To local surfers, it's just "the cove."

Watching Dave from the beach, you thought surfing looked effortless. When he asked if you were ready to go out, you eagerly grabbed a board and splashed in. But when you got your first mouthful of bitter salt water and felt the power of a wave as it plunged you to the bottom, you realized that it wasn't going to be so easy after all. You didn't let that stop you, though, from paddling out every day after that on the board your uncle lent you.

*Turn to page 72.*

You jump out of the field and the path of the writhing snakes. "They've come out of their holes!" the man shouts. "They know better than to get crushed when the quake comes. And listen. Hear any birds?"

You listen. You don't. The day is extremely still. You can tell it's going to be a scorcher, too.

"I'd say anytime between now and sunset the earth's going to shake!" the man says, and as he speaks you finally realize who he is. He's Earthquake Joe. Your uncle has told you about him—he was once a geology professor at the local university. He now lives all alone in the hills, devoting his time to predicting the next big quake.

"This morning, one of my pigs bit off her brother's tail. And my dog's been whimpering and barking at the sun since dawn," Joe says. His voice becomes serious as he goes on. "But what really worries me is that oil rig out there. See this fault line?" He points out a jagged line that extends out of the hills and disappears where the cliffs meet the ocean. "That fault goes straight out to sea. They built that oil rig right alongside it."

You follow his gaze out to the towering oil rig shimmering under the hot sun. "When the quake hits, that rig's going to fill with volatile gas and blow sky high. Anybody on it will be a goner. And the oil spill that comes after will kill the birds, poison the fish and sea mammals, and put a black slime on the beaches for years to come."

*Turn to page 76.*

You think Leia turns a little pale when she sees the shark bites, but it's hard to tell under her dark tan and tough exterior. She pushes her hair off her forehead, gives you a hard look, and shrugs. "Haven't seen Jorge in a while. But listen, gremmie, get that shark-eaten board outta here before it brings us all bad luck."

You stalk out of the surf shop, muttering, "Gremmie, huh?" Gremmie is slang for a young—and immature—surfer. As you get back on your bike, you can't help feeling that the Surf Monkeys know more than they're saying, but you're too intimidated to go back and press them.

There's one last place you can check for Jorge—his aunt Maria's house. Jorge was born in a small, very poor town in Baja, Mexico. You don't know his last name, and you don't know where his parents live. From hints he dropped, you think they may have returned to Mexico. Jorge somehow managed to stay with Maria and go to school.

You drop off the boards at your uncle's house and ride ten minutes to the little turquoise house where Maria lives. She opens the door, her two young children, Jorge's cousins, eyeing you curiously from behind her legs. You struggle with your second-year Spanish. "*¿Hola, ha visto Jorge hoy?*" you say, asking if she's seen Jorge today.

"*No, hoy no. No vuelve anoche.*" He didn't return last night, she says, and adds in English, "Wasn't he with you?"

*Go on to the next page.*

You shake your head and ask if you can take a look in Jorge's room. Maria motions you in, looking worried. His room is dark and, as usual, a mess. You check the closet and the bathtub. No wet suit. So Jorge did go surfing—or intended to. On your way out, you notice a picture of Jorge grinning up at you from his desk. You stuff it into your pocket. It might come in handy.

*Turn to page 121.*

"Sorry, Jorge," Leia breaks in. "But now is the time. We're right here, and these trolls are tied up—there's no one to stop us from shutting down the rig now."

"Hold on, Leia," you say. "You're not serious."

"Listen," Leia insists, "there could be a spill tomorrow. No one's on the rig right now. We're out here, let's go for it."

"In this fog, after two narrow escapes already?" you object. "You're really pushing it."

"That's what surfing's all about, dog," Leia replies with fierce conviction. "Finding the edge."

You grab the throttle, just to make sure no one takes it away, and start to move forward. You glance around the boat at the other Surf Monkeys, who seem undecided. You feel that you have veto power over this idea—not to mention the wheel of the motorboat. Should you tell Leia enough is enough and turn the boat around? Or do you think she's right after all? Either way, you must act decisively.

*If you decide to head for the oil rig, turn to page 63.*

*If you head the boat for shore, turn to page 106.*

Bethany turns to you and says, "So what do *you* think of that oil rig?"

"It's pretty ugly," you answer. "It ought to be illegal to build those things."

The Surf Monkeys eye each other. Leia looks at you closely and says, "So, gremmie... you interested in becoming a Surf Monkey?"

You hardly expected such an invitation from the Surf Monkeys. You're thrilled at first, but then you remember your misgivings about them. They seem especially nervous and secretive tonight. But then again, they really know how to surf, and they do make the best surfboards in town.

"Um, well, yeah, sure... I guess so," is all you manage to stammer.

"Well, think about it," Leia says. "If you're interested, meet us at the lighthouse at midnight tonight. We'll give you a little initiation ritual." As you ride back to your uncle's house, you ponder Leia's invitation. If you get on the Surf Monkeys' good side, they might be able to help you find Jorge.

On the other hand, you're still wary of them. They might just be a distraction. And you wonder what kind of initiation they have in store for you.

---

*If you decide to join the Surf Monkeys,
turn to page 50.*

*If you decide to keep searching for Jorge by
yourself, turn to page 107.*

The Surf Monkeys consider the spot their private surf zone, but you decide to risk their ire, hoping to hear something about Jorge. As expected, they give you the cold shoulder when you attempt to make conversation.

Their surfing etiquette isn't the best either—every time you catch a wave, you find one of the Surf Monkeys bearing down behind you, surfing dangerously close. "Hey, off my wave, gremmie!" Tommy shouts. He aims his board straight at you on a steep wave, forcing you to pull out.

But you hang in there doggedly as the afternoon goes on. The swell picks up, giving you a chance to show what you can do on some highly rippable tubes.

*Turn to page 33.*

# 12

A moment later, Mai and Annie are gesticulating from the dock at the useless craft and arguing over what to do. As silently as you can, you pull yourself out of the water and onto the dock. The two workers are too preoccupied with rage over the upside-down boat to notice you.

But Jorge does. His eyes light up, and you exchange a wordless message of understanding about what to do next. You hastily untie him and the two of you charge across the deck at the oil workers.

They start to turn, but as you'd hoped, they're too surprised to react very fast. A pair of hearty shoves sends them flying off the dock and into the water, where they splash around, coughing, sputtering, and cursing.

You and Jorge dash up the gangplank. You get to the top just in time to pull the lever. The gangplank lifts up and away just as the two workers pull themselves back up onto the dock.

As Mai and Annie get to their feet, they shake their fists at you and scream, "You'll pay for this!" They say some more things that cause you to blush, but you yank Jorge out of earshot.

"You think they'll survive down there?" you ask him.

"They'll get a bit cold—but that's all right, it'll sharpen them up," Jorge replies.

"As long as they don't cause any more trouble for us," you say.

*Turn to page 48.*

You stay where you are behind the storage tank, hoping for another chance to rescue Jorge.

Mai's partner Annie crosses to a gearbox near the dock and pulls a lever. You hear machinery grinding and figure it must be the gangplank being lowered. There's a grunt as Mai gives Jorge another push toward the edge of the rig. With panic, you realize only a few moments are left before Jorge will be in the launch on the way to the supertanker.

The crucial link is the launch—suddenly you have an idea. Keeping the storage tank between yourself and the oil workers, you move to a guard-rail at the edge of the rig. After a brief moment contemplating the huge swells below, you climb onto the rail—and dive. It seems a long time until you hit the water. When you do, you go deep, struggle up to the surface for a breath, then dive back down and swim underwater toward the dock.

*Turn to page 34.*

Finally, with a free moment to savor your joy at finding Jorge alive, you also have a chance to find out what's going on. "What the heck are you doing out on this rig anyway?" you demand. "I just spent two days thinking you were shark bait."

Jorge's eyes fall. "I was recruited by the Surf Monkeys," he says. "They needed someone small."

In response to your questioning look, he goes on to explain the whole story. It turns out that the Surf Monkeys' opposition to the oil rig was more than just talk. They'd been trying to stop its construction for years. They found out it was alongside an earthquake fault. If there was a big quake, or even if a worker fell asleep at the controls, it could result in a massive oil spill.

*Turn to page 102.*

"All right," you agree. "Catch some big ones for me."

Dave gives you a wink as he heads out the door. "We'll be feasting on smoked salmon for the rest of the summer."

You fiddle with the radio dials, listening in on the various broadcasts. Your eyelids are just starting to get heavy again when you home in on a voice saying, "This is *Alpha Yankee* calling *Polar Bear*, over."

You recognize the names from the local news. *Alpha Yankee* is the oil rig being built offshore, and *Polar Bear* is a giant supertanker that's been in the harbor for the past couple of days.

"We read you, *Alpha Yankee*. Go ahead," the ship returns.

*Go on to the next page.*

"When do you sail for Valdez? Over."

"Tomorrow morning, zero three two niner, over."

"Well, we've got some extra cargo for you. We've had a little trouble with some locals. They don't seem to like our rig very much. Anyhow, we have a surfer here who says he'd like to try that cold surf up around the Arctic Circle. We picked him up last night."

"I read you. Why don't you escort your guest out when we get underway? We'll be watching for him, over."

"Roger. Over and out."

*Turn to page 111.*

"For your initiation as a Surf Monkey, you have a choice," Leia says. "You can either take a midnight ride on the Big Swell—"

"Wait a minute," you interrupt. "The Big Swell doesn't even run anymore." The Big Swell is an abandoned roller coaster at the amusement park on the edge of town, shut down years ago after a bad accident.

"It does when we want it to," Bethany announces. The other Surf Monkeys glance at each other with nervous amusement under their shaggy hair.

"But if you don't like roller coasters," Leia continues, "there's an authentic west ground swell tonight. Perfect for a little nighttime surfing—under the pier."

"You mean shoot the pier? At night?" you ask incredulously. You know it's dangerous enough during the daytime to try to surf between the barnacle-encrusted pilings of the pier. The best that anyone who misses can hope for is to get torn up good by the sharp barnacles—instead of flying headlong into a pylon and drowning.

Leia nods slowly. "Shoot the pier at night. Show us you can really surf. Unfortunately there's not much moonlight to show you the way. You'll have to use a little radar." The other Surf Monkeys chuckle softly.

*Go on to the next page.*

You pause and rub your chin, considering your choices. The last time you saw the old roller coaster, it looked pretty rusty. But shooting the pier at night is really risky, too.

The Surf Monkeys wait for your decision.

---

*If you decide to take the roller coaster ride, turn to page 30.*

*If you'd rather try to prove your surfing prowess by shooting the pier in the dark, turn to page 110.*

# 20

The swell is growing, starting to curl behind you. You're picking up speed as you grip the sides of your board and make the jump to your feet. You're racing down the slope of the wave now, barely able to make out the dark pier ahead. Then you see them—glowing plankton at the base of the pilings. You shoot between a set of pilings, race under the pier, and weave through another set. You heave an enormous sigh of relief as you come out the other side unscathed.

*Turn to page 22.*

# 22

Leia is right behind you. "Awesome, gremmie!" she cries, coming up to fist bump you. The other Surf Monkeys grin and slap you on the back as you paddle back to shore.

Everyone is in high spirits at having carried out the deadly maneuver, and they careen into town to celebrate. Still intoxicated with adrenaline, you roll along with them.

*Go on to the next page.*

As it gets late, the Surf Monkeys begin to glance at each other nervously. "Pouch time," Tommy says, meaning he's going to bed.

"Same time tomorrow night at the lighthouse," Leia calls to you as they head off. "Be there."

You stumble out into the dark streets, ready to head home yourself. As you turn a corner, you nearly run into a large man coming out of a beach-front pub called the Oiled Gull. He lurches toward you, clamping his huge hand on your shoulder. You gasp and look away, startled by the burn scars disfiguring his face.

*Turn to page 84.*

You make the rounds of the police station and everywhere else you can think of in town, but no one has seen Jorge. You keep expecting him to pop up any minute with his wicked grin and drag you down to the cove to surf. But by sunset there's still no sign of him. You begin to feel panicky. Now you wish Dave hadn't run off before you had a chance to ask his advice.

Dejectedly you go home and cook up a hot dog for dinner. Later you fall asleep in front of the TV, waking to the sound of waves in your head and the laugh track of the station's late-night reruns. Suddenly you remember your midnight meeting with the Surf Monkeys.

A strong, hot wind is blowing, making your hair stand on end with static electricity. The surf pounds far below you on the rocks as you cross the top of the bluff on your way to the lighthouse. You think of how quiet the Surf Monkeys became when you first showed them Jorge's board. *They* must *know more than they are letting on. It's time to ask them about Jorge's disappearance*, you decide.

You arrive at the lighthouse a little after midnight and climb the stairs slowly, feeling unsure about your involvement with the Surf Monkeys. As you reach the top, you hear the sound of a fierce argument. It's Leia and Tommy. You stop, hesitating outside the slightly open door.

*Turn to page 62.*

Intuition tells you there's more to be learned at the cove. After all, the last thing Jorge did was go surfing.

You make your way to the wreck of the old freighter and find a place to sit in the shade of the rusty hull. Even as you wonder if you'll ever see Jorge again, you keep having a strange sensation of his presence—the feeling that he's somewhere nearby.

"Jorge, the ocean spirit," you muse aloud. Where is he? Every time a wave crashes on the shore, you think you hear his crazy laugh.

All at once your eyes lock onto some graffiti scratched into the rusty steel hull of the freighter: WRECK THE RIG, it says—and it's written in Jorge's distinctive style!

Your mind races back to the Surf Monkeys on the beach yesterday, asking what you thought of the rig. And the equipment you found in the hidden room of the lighthouse—but what does it all mean?

You're confused, and the heat is starting to make you feel dizzy.

Maybe a swim will clear your head. You leave the hull of the freighter, edge out on a rocky ledge, and dive into a clear, deep pool. After swimming out a ways, you float on your back in the swells, your eyes closed.

Just then something brushes beneath you. Instantly you panic at the thought of another shark. You open your eyes to see three fins arcing through the water just a few feet away.

*Turn to page 87.*

# 26

When you reach the edge of town, the dry Baja desert starts. After a few hours you reach a small town with a harbor. You bargain with a local fisherman to take you out to a deserted island off the coast.

The fisherman drops you off at a beautiful bay on the western side of the island. The biggest and most perfect waves you've ever seen are breaking offshore.

"That's real," Leia breathes, in a low, awestruck voice.

You spend the next two days surfing, camping out, and eating the barbecued lobster and fish you've caught every night. But on the morning of the third day you tell Leia, "I've got to get back to the mainland. Jorge's from Baja, and I want to look for him."

Leia brushes her hair out of her eyes and gives you a pat on the shoulder. "Chill out, gremmie. You're not going to find Jorge out here."

"Where is he then?" you demand.

"The oil workers on the rig back at the cove are holding him prisoner," she responds nonchalantly.

Seeing the stricken look on your face, she goes on. "Listen, there's nothing we can do about it. We'll head back in a few days, when things have cooled down, and find out what's happened to him."

"No way," you say sternly. "I'm going back now."

*Turn to page 43.*

You step through the doorway into the dimly lit circular room just as the Surf Monkeys are getting up to leave. When they see you, Lance curses under his breath. The rest look at Leia. Leia steps toward you, trying to act cool.

"Hey gremmie, where have you been?" she says. "We've been waiting for you. We're just about to take off for a little surfing in Mexico. Want to come?"

You stare open-mouthed for a minute, struck by two thoughts. First, you're amazed at how fast Leia can shift gears. But second, you remember that Jorge's from Baja. You may be able to pick up some clues about his disappearance there.

"Think fast, gremmie," Leia says. "We're leaving in an hour. I hear there's going to be a heavy swell down there, caused by an earthquake off the coast of Ecuador. It'll probably be the best surfing of your life."

Your mind races. After the conversation you just overheard, you're not at all sure you can trust the Surf Monkeys. On the other hand, this may be your best chance to look for clues about Jorge. And, as Leia says, the surfing wouldn't be bad, either.

---

*If you think you should stay and look for Jorge here, turn to page 38.*

*If you decide to go to Baja, turn to page 59.*

# 30

"I'll do the Big Swell," you say. You've read somewhere that riding a roller coaster is actually safer than crossing a street. If the Big Swell has had one accident, it probably won't have another for a long time.

You and the Surf Monkeys pack into Leia's van for the ride down to the abandoned amusement park. Quickly you hop the chain link fence. The Big Swell looms high above you. Its old peeling cars sit eerily still at the bottom. "I hate to tell you guys, but this old rust heap doesn't look like it's taking anyone for a ride," you say.

Leia gives you a knowing smile and says, "You haven't seen Surf Monkey magic yet, gremmie."

She disappears inside the control house with a box of tools. For the next few minutes you hear her cursing and dropping wrenches in the dark. Then you hear a grinding noise. The cars on the track start to vibrate.

Leia emerges triumphantly, covered with grease. "Pick your car, gremmie!" she shouts.

*Turn to page 91.*

The gangplank leading from the dock to the rig platform is pulled up, but you find a utility ladder. Slowly and carefully you climb it, listening to the rig's vibration. It must be pumping oil.

You reach the top of the ladder and silently clamber onto the platform deck. The first thing you see is a bearded man fast asleep in the sun, snoring loudly. He looks peaceful enough, until you notice the gun lying at his side. You tiptoe over, carefully lift the gun, and toss it into the ocean far below. Hoping he doesn't wake up, you move on, feeling better now about taking a tour of the rig.

It's much bigger than you'd imagined, a vast maze of catwalks and ladders connecting several stories of drilling rigs, cranes, control rooms, storage tanks, and living quarters. As you work your way along the walkways, it seems that the rig is in full operation with no one at the controls.

You're about to round a corner when you hear a clanking sound. You let out a soft whistle. The scraping stops. You whistle again and hear a muffled cry. You take a deep breath and turn the corner. Chained to a crane, gagged and blindfolded, is Jorge!

Not knowing whether to laugh or cry, you rush over and untie his gag and blindfold. Jorge works his jaw up and down a few times, then looks at you and hisses, "What took you so long?! Where's Leia?"

"Leia is in Mexico, surfing," you reply. "Stay put. I'll be right back."

*Turn to page 92.*

Then, at about sunset, you hear angry voices behind you. A fight is breaking out between two Surf Monkeys. You turn just in time to see Bethany hit Tommy with a solid punch in the nose. Blood pours from Tommy's nose, but he just splashes it with salt water and comes back at Bethany, dragging her off her board and into the water. They continue to splash and shout and throw punches at each other.

Suddenly you see a dark fin knifing through the water—headed straight for Bethany! You break into a cold sweat. Sharks, you recall, can instantly smell blood miles away through the water.

"Shark!" you manage to shout.

But the Surf Monkeys don't hear you. They continue their furious battle. You don't have a second to waste. The shark starts to circle the surfers. Grabbing a piece of driftwood, you silently paddle as close to the shark as you dare and raise the wood above your head. The shark makes a darting turn, and for a brief moment you are eye to eye with it. Then you bring the wood down hard on its flat, primitive head.

*Turn to page 47.*

# 34

You surface just in time to see the rig workers and Jorge at the top of the gangplank. After a couple of breaths, you dive again, gauging the distance to the launch. You come up next to it, grab the gunwale, and timing it with the wave, you heave. The small boat flips up on its side. Just as it turns over and starts to come down on top of you, you go underwater again.

Now you swim to the rear of the dock. With your head barely above water, you have to wait only a few seconds before you hear a string of oaths from Mai. He and Annie have reached the bottom of the gangplank and discovered the capsized launch.

*Turn to page 12.*

When you arrive at the fire, Leia holds her hand up for a high five. "Good work, gremmie. You saved these two trolls from becoming lunch meat."

Each of the other Surf Monkeys comes up to shake your hand as you sit down. They saw the whole thing from the beach, and it's changed their attitude toward you. As you hang out, you talk about the shark for a while; then the conversation turns to the new oil rig being built a few miles offshore.

*Turn to page 9.*

Suddenly both you and Jorge are thrown to the ground. You cling desperately to the planks as the pier continues to ripple and shake for what seems like ages. You're sure you're going to get thrown into the ocean, but the old pier flexes with the jolts of the quake.

As quickly as it began, the earthquake is over. You and Jorge struggle to your feet. Everything is strangely still. Then you hear a loud roar and see a flash. Jorge grabs you by the shoulder and points offshore. You look just in time to see a giant ball of fire envelop the oil rig.

You slowly wipe an arm across your forehead. "I'm sure glad we shut down that rig last night. Well, that should take care of oil drilling around here for a long time."

"Not to mention those hungry sharks," Jorge remarks.

You stare back at the now-calm sea. "The folks back home in Indiana are never going to believe this," you say, shaking your head.

### The End

"Sorry, I can't go anywhere right now," you say to the Surf Monkeys.

"Too bad," Leia starts to say. "You're gonna miss—"

"I've got to stay and look for my friend, Jorge," you interrupt coldly, emphasizing the word *friend*.

A sudden silence falls over the room, punctuated only by the crashing waves below. Leia seems to regard you with a mixture of anger, guilt, and respect.

You return Leia's stare and go on, "Look, I know Jorge's in some kind of trouble. Just tell me what's going on. Where is he?"

There's a long pause. The Surf Monkeys glance back and forth at one another. Then Leia looks at you and says, "We can't tell you everything, but... Jorge's on the high seas. The local pirates got him. Just head due west, you'll find him. He's not far."

Lance grabs Leia by the elbow. "That's enough," he says. "Let's go."

Leia rips her arm away and glares at Lance. Then she puts her hand on your shoulder and says, "Good luck, gremmie." The Surf Monkeys leave.

*Go on to the next page.*

You walk out of the lighthouse, confused and angry. It seems as though the Surf Monkeys are just playing games with you.

"Due west, huh?" you say to yourself. You gaze out to sea. The lighthouse beam is just swinging around, grazing across the dark, windblown water. It briefly illuminates the oil rig standing a mile out in the ocean.

A thought comes to you. *That rig is the only thing between here and Japan. And it's due west.*

Leia said "pirates" had gotten Jorge. But there are no pirates out there, just the people on the rig. You flash back to the man who grabbed you coming out of the pub last night. Could there be a connection? Could Jorge be a prisoner of the workers on the rig?

*Turn to page 70.*

*There must be a way to stop the light from turning long enough to signal*, you think.

A screwdriver has been left on the floor. You pick it up and wait for the light to swing around. Just at the moment it's pointing at the oil rig, you jam the screwdriver into the gears. The giant mirrors shudder to a stop. The lighthouse beam is at a standstill, shooting out across the water straight to the rig.

Now you look for the light switch. It's conveniently located on a box near your feet. You click it off. Suddenly everything's dark. Then, using the switch, you click out your message in Morse code: JORGE, ARE YOU OUT THERE?

For a moment nothing happens. But in another moment a tiny flash of light from very far out comes back across the water: three short, three long, three short: S.O.S.

There's nothing more. Your heart is beating fast. At last you've found Jorge. And he's alive. But how are you going to get to him?

The only vessel you have is your surfboard. Paddling out to the rig is a dangerous venture. You will have to cross the shipping lanes and contend with strong tides. You might not make it all the way out there, and even if you do, the rig workers might not take kindly to your presence if they find you.

You pull the screwdriver out of the gears, and the mirrors start up again. You've got to get out to the rig right now. Jorge's life may depend on it.

*Turn to page 67.*

# 42

After a few hours you wake. You try to go back to sleep, but you keep thinking about all the surfers out in the water with those starved sharks. You pad downstairs to find Jorge awake and sipping a glass of orange juice.

"I'm ravenous," he says. "Let's go down to the Pier Inn and get some breakfast."

When you get to the restaurant, a little shack built at the end of the pier, you're relieved to see there are no surfers out on the water—it's a totally flat day with hardly a ripple. "I'm still worried about those sharks," you say to Jorge as the two of you grab a window booth.

You order up a gigantic breakfast. Just as you're taking your first forkful of scrambled eggs, you start to feel a tremor. You and Jorge look at each other, then wordlessly run outside, wondering how the pier can be shaking when there isn't any surf.

A strange rumble is coming from the shore. You glance toward town to see a row of houses lifting up in a wavelike motion. It's the strangest thing you've ever seen.

"¡*Terremoto*!" Jorge shouts.

"What?" you scream back, grabbing onto a railing as the same wave motion travels up the pier, lifting the planks. You feel as if you're on a giant roller coaster.

"Earthquake!"

*Turn to page 36*.

Leia gives you an apologetic smile. "No can do. The fisherman's not coming back for another four days. So, unless you want to swim, I guess you're stuck here with the most awesome waves on the coast. Why not just enjoy them?"

You turn and stalk off, feeling totally helpless. The next four days in surf paradise are the most miserable of your life.

**The End**

Something tells you that the Surf Monkeys can help you rescue Jorge. Bright and early the next morning, you grab your skateboard and ride down to the surf shop. The door's still locked, but you can hear activity in a back room. You knock loudly, and pretty soon Leia sticks her head out. Her expression tenses when she sees you, but she walks over to open the door.

"We're closed, gremmie," she says, obviously peeved you failed to show up last night.

"We've got to talk, Leia," you say, looking her straight in the eye as you push past her into the shop.

"What's up?" Leia demands.

"Jorge's a prisoner out on the oil rig. I overheard some guy from the rig talking to the captain of the *Polar Bear* on the ship-to-shore radio. They're planning to ship Jorge to Alaska—tonight. We've got to help him."

Leia looks startled, then an expression of concern crosses her face. *Maybe she does care about Jorge*, you think. She motions you into the back room, where five of the Surf Monkeys are hanging out. Two of them are using sanders to shape a surfboard set on sawhorses in the middle of the room.

*Go on to the next page.*

Leia walks over, unplugs the sander, and announces, "Gremmie here says the rig workers are planning to put Jorge on a tanker to Alaska tonight." She stops for a moment, letting the news sink in. "I guess they really want to teach us a lesson. We're going to have to intercept them if we ever want to see Jorge again."

"Wait a minute," Lance objects. "Why should we put ourselves on the line for Jorge? He knew the risks when he went out there."

*Turn to page 113.*

# 46

Your arms feel as heavy as iron. Your lungs ache, and your eyes sting from the salt. Your feet have long been numb from the cold water.

It seems like hours have gone by when suddenly the cement pilings of the rig loom up before you. You're shocked at how giant the rig is. It seems as high as a ten-story building, and there doesn't seem to be any way to get onto it. A little more paddling brings you to a dock. A small launch is tied up there, but the gangplank has been pulled up.

Finally you find an anchor chain. You tie your board's leash to the chain, and with what little strength you have left in your arms, you're able to shimmy up the chain. Gasping, you pull yourself over the top railing of the rig.

Now you're standing in a floodlight in front of an enormous tower of churning machinery. Before you can see anything more, you hear the sound of voices. Quickly you duck behind a large storage tank just as a man and a woman emerge from a doorway on the other side of the rig—with Jorge!

Your timing has been perfect. Jorge's hands are tied in front of him, and the two people are dragging him toward the gangplank. At least he's alive. When the floodlights fall on their faces you recognize the man who grabbed you outside the pub.

*Turn to page 112.*

The shark reacts fast, diving suddenly under your board. You scramble to keep your legs out of the way, holding your breath until you see its shadowy form under the water turn and head back out to sea. "Paddle in!" you shout to the two Surf Monkeys, who have finally realized what's happening.

"I've never seen a shark this close to shore before," Tommy says, still gasping, as you reach the shore. He looks pretty shook up.

"For real!" gasps Bethany. "Did you see the size of that thing?"

"Seriously! Hey, thanks, gremmie," Tommy says, giving you a sidelong look of gratitude. "That was quick thinking."

You're shaken, too, but secretly proud of yourself. "No problem," you respond. "Just be careful where you bleed next time."

"Yeah, those sharks have a wicked sense of smell," Bethany says.

The two Surf Monkeys seem to have forgotten their fight. "Come on up and get warm," Tommy says, jerking his head toward the driftwood bonfire some of the other Surf Monkeys have built near the shipwreck.

*Turn to page 35.*

"I don't think they will," Jorge says. "Chances are someone will check in on them within the hour. They were the only ones on this platform. They didn't want to risk the other workers finding out what they planned to do with me."

"That was a pretty close call, buddy," you say to Jorge.

Jorge gives a long, slow nod. Then suddenly his eyes regain their sparkle. He gives you a slap on the shoulder, flashes his old wicked grin, and says, "¡Madre mía! I sure didn't want to go surfing in Alaska in this weather."

You laugh, wrap an arm around his shoulders, and reply, "Hey, I thought you told me you could surf anywhere."

"At least I've still got my wet suit on," he says, looking down at his battered rubber suit. "Or most of it."

*Turn to page 15.*

Jorge nods. "Yeah, the Surf Monkeys were pretty serious. I thought we were doing the right thing, too. But when a rig worker pointed a gun at me, I knew things had gone too far.

"As a matter of fact," Jorge continues, "I was almost forced onto a tanker to Alaska. But just before the rig workers were going to take me out, I got away and hid long enough to miss it."

"Sounds like a close call," you comment, clipping through the last of Jorge's heavy chains. "But what's important now is that we get off this rig before the earthquake hits."

Jorge grabs your arm. "First we better shut this baby down. If it's a big quake, the rig could blow oil all over the beach."

The ocean sparkles far below as you follow Jorge down a catwalk, keeping as close to the walls as possible. Jorge has obviously learned something about the rig during his stay, because he takes you directly to a door that says CONTROL ROOM.

*Turn to page 61.*

# 50

At midnight, you ride out to the point and climb the stairs of the lighthouse. You figure you've got nothing to lose by joining the Surf Monkeys, and there's a chance they'll eventually lead you to Jorge. It's a clear night, and as you go higher, you glimpse the lighthouse beam stretching far out over the vast ocean.

You find the Surf Monkeys sitting cross-legged around a lantern in the small circular room at the top. Leia jumps up to give you a vigorous high five. "All right! So you're ready to become a Surf Monkey."

You sit down, and they begin to explain their philosophy to you. "We live for the waves," Leia says, a note of reverence in her voice. "The waves are our life."

"Word," Tommy agrees.

"The waves are free, right?" Leia goes on. "They come from the ocean. But there are people who think they own them. We're here to save the ocean from those who are busy destroying it. Our pledge is, 'The ocean is all. All for the ocean.'"

*Go on to the next page.*

Leia looks at you expectantly. Suddenly you realize you're supposed to repeat the pledge, which you try to do with enthusiasm.

"Just so," she says. "Now you're a Surf Monkey—*almost*."

"You still have to do the initiation," Lance chimes in, an evil smile creasing his face.

*Turn to page 18.*

# 52

Jorge pauses, and you exchange a long, silent look. "I know this was a dumb thing to do," he says finally. "But it seemed like a good idea at the time. I don't know, I guess I just wanted to be accepted by the Surf Monkeys."

"Who are on their way to Baja now," you remark. "First they give you the most dangerous job—then they leave you dangling out here. Some friends."

Jorge just shakes his head in silent agreement. By now it's nearly dawn. You're exhausted and suggest that you rest and wait for daylight before the two of you paddle back. In a matter of moments, you and Jorge are sound asleep.

*Turn to page 60.*

Everybody seeks cover, stumbling and cursing. Then one man says, "What about the rig? There's nobody out there! It's gonna blow if it doesn't get shut down!"

Another man says, "Well, I sure ain't going out there. Tough luck for that kid..." Seeing you, he abruptly breaks off.

Finally the trembling stops. There's a strange silence in the wake of the roar. The men who were talking about the rig look at each other. Then they look at you.

Suddenly you have a horrible feeling that you know where Jorge is. And you know you're the only one who's going to help him.

You race out of the pub and run all the way down to the marina. Your Uncle Dave has a friend who keeps an old motorboat there, and you happen to know where the engine key is hidden.

You manage to get the boat started and headed out into the open water without anyone asking questions. Steering toward the oil rig, you check behind you to make sure no one is following.

*Turn to the next page.*

## 54

Suddenly there's a huge roar. You turn back just in time to see the oil rig engulfed in a tower of flame. You're overcome by a feeling of horror, but you keep on your course toward the rig. Nothing can stop you from reaching Jorge. You just hope there's not another explosion.

Soon you can feel the heat of the fire. The flames are spreading. Then, with even greater horror, you realize the ocean itself is on fire. A sheen of flaming oil is pouring from the rig. Your heart sinks. The rig and the ocean all around it are completely engulfed in fire. The whole world seems to be on the brink of apocalypse.

*Turn to page 114.*

Jorge will be on his way to Alaska in a matter of minutes. This may be your last chance to rescue him. You peer around the edge of the storage tank and watch the woman named Annie pull a lever on a gearbox. A moment later, the gangplank starts to lower to the dock.

"Let's go," Mai says, giving Jorge another shove.

This is it. As soon as they're at the edge of the platform, you dash out from behind the tank. You close in on the two rig workers, picking up speed, ready to knock them off the edge of the rig. But just before you get there, Mai happens to turn. Even caught off guard, he has enough time to jerk an elbow up, catching you on the jaw and sending you sprawling to the deck.

You shake off the blow and manage to get to your feet, only to find yourself staring down the barrel of a gun. You summon your most commanding voice and say, "Kidnapping is a pretty serious crime. I doubt you want to lose your jobs over this."

The two rig workers stare at you in disbelief for a few seconds. Then Mai breaks into guttural laughter and says, "Fact is, we'll lose our jobs if we don't get rid of you troublemakers."

"I guess we got another guest for the cruise," Annie observes.

Cocking his gun at you, Mai adds, "Sorry we don't have time to give you a tour of the rig, but your ship has come in. Hope you packed your toothbrush."

*Turn to page 81.*

You look back to see that the other Surf Monkeys have also caught the wake. One of them lets out a bloodcurdling howl. The enormous ship looms up behind you like a giant black planet, filling the whole sky. You crouch into the wave, going for speed, and the ship somehow passes behind you. You and the other Surf Monkeys have made it! You pull out of the wake, breathing hard.

Just when you think you're safe, you hear the sound of an outboard motor. "Get down and stay still," Leia hisses.

Everyone lies flat on their boards. The motor comes closer, but the boat is still invisible in the white fog. When it emerges, you see it's headed in the direction of the tanker disappearing into the fog. You also catch sight of three dark silhouettes seated in the boat. The figure in the middle is smaller than the other two. It's got to be Jorge!

*Turn to the next page.*

# 58

"Go!" Leia whispers. Everyone paddles smoothly and silently to intercept the boat. You time your approach to the starboard side so that, as you reach the boat, you've got your surf leash wrapped around both hands. You kneel on your board and slip the leash around the neck of one of the dark silhouettes, pulling the man over backward into the water.

Bethany and Tommy come to your aid as the man swings wildly at you in the water. Before long you've got him wrapped up in your surf leash, and you heave him back into the boat. Meanwhile, Leia has dealt with the second figure. She's already in the boat, using the anchor chain to tie the person up. You leave Bethany and Tommy to get your man tied up, too, while you tend to the smaller figure. Your heart jumps when you see you were right—it's Jorge!

*Turn to page 122.*

"I'm in," you say, accepting Leia's invitation to Baja.

"All right!" Leia exclaims. "Everyone meet at my house in an hour."

You race home, pack some clothes, and grab your board. Uncle Dave is still up the coast fishing, so you leave him a note saying you'll be back in a few days. As an old surfer, he'll understand a spur-of-the-moment trip to Baja.

The other Surf Monkeys are already at Leia's house when you arrive. You all pile into her van.

"Everybody cough up five bucks for gas," Leia announces. You all grumble as you reach into your pockets for money, then Leia heads the van south, down the coastal highway. You've had a long day, and the rocking of the van soon lulls you into a deep sleep.

You wake just as the sun's coming up the next morning. You're crossing the border into Mexico, and it's a very different landscape. The wide highways and green lawns of Southern California are replaced by dry, dusty roads peppered with small buildings strung with bright flags. People sell colorful blankets and ceramic skulls under white tents to avoid the heat. Children run through the streets selling toys. Donkeys painted with zebra stripes pull carts of tourists over the streets, and trucks piled with loudspeakers rove through the streets blaring all types of music.

*Turn to page 26.*

# 60

You're awakened by a sudden jolt. It's broad daylight.

You stand up, remembering where you are, but are knocked back to the floor by another, even stronger jolt. Jorge is awake, too. He looks at you wildly and shouts, "It's an earthquake! We've got to shut the pump down or this whole rig's gonna blow!"

The two of you race into the control room. During his work on the rig, Jorge has managed to figure out how the pump works. He pulls the emergency lever, shutting down the whole system. You both race back outside. By now the rig is shaking violently. It begins to rock back and forth, groaning horribly.

"Holy moly!" you cry. "Is this the Big One?"

"Biggest one I've ever felt!" Jorge exclaims. He grabs your shoulder and turns you in the direction he's staring. The biggest swells you've ever seen are heading right for the rig.

"We have to get ashore," he shouts. "The rig will never survive waves this big!"

*Turn to page 108.*

After a quick search of the vast array of monitors and pressure gauges, you find what you're looking for: EMERGENCY SHUTDOWN. The red lever is behind a pane of glass. You smash the bolt cutters through the glass and pull the lever. A great moan comes from the rig as the machinery shudders to a halt. In the sudden quiet you can hear the sound of the waves breaking against the pilings far below.

You and Jorge slip out of the control room just in time to see the now-awake guard charging up the stairs toward you—and he's gripping a rifle.

"That's the only way down!" Jorge hisses.

"Except for this way," you say, looking over the railing to the ocean below.

Jorge gives you a furious glare. "What are we going to do—swim back?"

"Don't worry," you assure him. "I've got friends down there." You hope you're right as you start to climb over the railing.

*Turn to page 99.*

# 62

"But Jorge blew it," Leia says. "If he spills the beans, we'll all get locked up for a long time. And dudes, there's no surfing behind bars."

"But he's just a kid," Tommy protests. "We can't just leave him out there."

"We don't have a choice," Leia replies. "We gotta get out of town until the whole thing cools. I say we head down to Baja, do a little surfing out on Todos Santos Islands, and keep an eye on the newspapers until the coast is clear."

The other Surf Monkeys mumble their agreement. "What about the new kid?" Tommy persists.

"Forget about that gremmie," Leia says. "Let's get out of here. Meet at my house in an hour, and we'll head for the border."

You quickly crouch down behind the door. They know where Jorge is. But what does he know that's so dangerous? He and the Surf Monkeys are obviously involved in something illegal, but they're about to take off for Mexico. You've got to think fast. Should you step out, reveal that you've been listening to their conversation, and insist they tell you where Jorge is? Or should you remain concealed behind the door until they leave?

*If you decide to confront the Surf Monkeys, turn to page 29.*

*If you stay hidden until they leave, turn to page 71.*

"Okay, Leia, tell me which way to the rig," you say. "But no monkey business. We'll just find the emergency shutoff, pull it, and get out of there."

"It's a deal," Leia agrees. "Head the boat about thirty degrees to your left."

Soon the huge rig looms out of the fog. You cut the engine a hundred yards out, and Leia gears up with Tommy to paddle in. Bethany stays in the boat to keep an eye on the bound-and-gagged rig workers. You and Jorge sit up front, watching the rig appear and disappear in the racing fog.

Leia and Tommy return soon. Leia gives a big smile and a thumbs-up. "Piece of cake."

When you finally get back, you've never been so happy to hear the sound of the waves lapping the shore. It's just starting to get light. You tie up the boat, and leave your captives at the dock.

"When our friends get back, you surfers better watch out," one of them says.

"We'll see what the police have to say about that," Leia snaps back.

Jorge is sleeping so soundly you can't rouse him, so you and the Surf Monkeys stretch him out on a paddleboard and carry him back to your uncle's house. You tuck Jorge in on the couch, then after high fives all around with the Surf Monkeys, fall into bed yourself.

*Turn to page 42.*

You arrive back at the surf shop at midnight on the dot. All the Surf Monkeys except Lance are already there. Leia is handing out wet suits and paddleboards for each surfer. "Oh, and everybody grab a surf leash," she reminds you, taking one of the long plastic straps with Velcro anklets from the wall. "Let's go. We've got half an hour to get out to the main shipping channel."

You and the Surf Monkeys suit up and slip out into the dark streets, carrying the long paddleboards. A cat dashes in front of you, and you almost trip under the weight of the heavy board. It's strange to be walking through the deserted town in the middle of the night in a wet suit.

A block away from the beach you hear the low moan of foghorns. This isn't a good sign. You get to the boardwalk to find that a thick fog has come in and covered the water. You wonder how you're ever going to see the rig, but Leia doesn't appear concerned. You rub some wax on the old paddleboards, then head straight out through the chilly waves into the dense night fog.

You paddle farther and farther out with the Surf Monkeys. You can't see a thing through the fog, but Leia seems to know just where to go. "I get the feeling you guys have been out to the rig before," you remark to her, trying to keep up with her swift paddle.

*Turn to page 77.*

# 66

Just before the wave crashes on top of you, you manage to shoot out the front of the tube and pull out behind the wave. You and Jorge drop back and lie down on the board. Frantically you paddle over several more giant swells, narrowly avoiding being buried alive under tons of water.

Then, as suddenly as it started, there is a lull. The ocean is dead calm. You and Jorge have just enough strength to paddle in and drag yourselves onto the debris-strewn beach. Lying exhausted on the sand, you raise your head to see the giant rig tipping onto its side.

"Looks like the rig's a goner," you say.

"Yeah, but it didn't catch fire," Jorge observes. "I don't see any oil, either. I'm glad we shut those pumps down."

"For sure," you agree. After a pause, you add, "That was some monster wave."

Jorge gives you a sly look. "Yeah, but you should have waited for the one behind it. It was even bigger."

You use your last strength to punch Jorge in the ribs, but he just fends off the blow playfully and gives you one of his wicked smiles.

**The End**

You see an old paddleboard the Surf Monkeys have left leaning against a wall at the bottom of the lighthouse stairs. You grab it, hoping it still floats. Behind it, you find an old wet suit rotting in the corner. You throw your clothes off and pull on the rank black rubber suit. It's too big for you, but it will at least keep you from freezing.

You grab the paddleboard and make your way down the steep cliffs to the cove. The wind is really howling tonight. You can see the whitecaps in the lighthouse beam. At the beach you feel your way over the dark, slippery rocks. Something sharp cuts into your foot—a barnacle. You desperately wish you had your booties.

The salt water stings your cut foot as you wade into the ocean. The first wave comes in and rushes up around your waist, making you shudder. You take a deep breath, thrust the paddleboard in front of you, and throw yourself into the dark surf.

You know the cove well, but in the dark, wind-blown chop, it seems completely foreign. You paddle desperately to get out past the reef, trying to locate the familiar rocks jutting out of the water to guide you. But the chaotic high surf keeps breaking on top of you, and all you can do is paddle blindly into the waves.

*Turn to page 69.*

Somehow you manage to clear the reef without getting smashed on the rocks. Soon you're out in the open ocean, paddling down into giant, steep bowls and riding over enormous crests. You're able to keep your bearings by glancing back at the lighthouse. Every once in a while you catch a glimpse of the rig as the lighthouse beacon sweeps across it.

*Turn to page 46.*

# 70

You dash down the stairs to catch the Surf Monkeys, but they are gone. You'll have to figure it out on your own. But how can you confirm your suspicion?

The lighthouse beam sweeps by again and lights up the rig. Suddenly you have an idea. Maybe you can signal Jorge. Your uncle has told you about ships signaling each other at night using their lights to flash Morse code. And you learned Morse code when you downloaded a special app on your phone for a science project back in Indiana.

You've also heard the Surf Monkeys clapping messages to each other while sitting on their boards waiting for waves. Once you heard Jorge clap a message back to them—in Morse code. If he is on the rig, maybe you can flash him a message using the giant lighthouse beacon.

You look up at the lighthouse. There must be a way to get to the light itself. You go back up to the circular room and look around. For the first time, you notice a trapdoor in the ceiling. You pile up some old crates, climb on top of them, and push the door up. You then grab the ledge to pull yourself up into the space above. When you get there, you find you're in a tiny, glass-enclosed chamber where a single bulb is magnified by giant, revolving mirrors. You're in the heart of the lighthouse.

*Turn to page 40.*

You've heard enough to feel you can't trust the Surf Monkeys, so you stay hidden. As they prepare to leave, Leia says, "So long, Jorge. Don't light any matches out there." The others laugh halfheartedly.

When you're sure they've gone you come out from behind the door and look out at the ocean. The lighthouse beam, sweeping across the water, briefly illuminates the nearly completed oil rig standing about a mile out in the dark water.

You climb up into the circular room to see if the Surf Monkeys have left any clues behind. The room is dark. You stumble over the lantern, knocking a few loose bricks out of the wall when you fall against it. Eventually you find a book of matches in the corner and manage to light the lantern.

You survey the room in the dim yellow light. Starting to replace the bricks you knocked out, you notice there's a hole in the wall. You shine the lantern into the dark opening. To your surprise, there's another room on the other side.

You pull out more bricks and squeeze through the opening. By the lantern light, you find a whole array of equipment—diving suits, tanks, blow-torches, wrenches, and a few gallons of gasoline. Something about the equipment strikes you as sinister.

You pick up a map lying nearby. Tucking it into your pants, you climb out of the room, seal up the bricks behind you, and leave the lighthouse for home.

*Turn to page 117.*

Day after day, week after week, you learned how to judge the shape of the waves, where to take off, and how to drop into the clear green tubes as they roared toward the beach. When you closed your eyes each night you were lulled to sleep by the motion of the waves still rolling around in your inner ear. Your hair grew long and tangled and became bleached by the sun and salt water. Your nose was permanently peeled. Even your bed was perpetually filled with sand. You felt more at home on the waves than on dry land, and you couldn't believe you'd ever been able to live so far from the ocean.

Jorge was one of the first friends you made here. He paddled right up to you after a particularly embarrassing wipeout and said, "Keep your eyes on the shore when you're taking off. That way you won't get confused by the motion of the waves."

It turned out to be good advice, and the two of you started hanging out. Jorge is a quick and versatile athlete, and he has a wicked smile and sense of humor to go along with it. He can surf on just about anything—he can even do a flip on his surfboard. Soon, with his help, you become one of the better surfers at the cove.

*Turn to page 75.*

# 74

On the way down the mountain you can't stop thinking about what Earthquake Joe said about Leia. She seemed aloof and secretive to you, but from what Earthquake Joe said, Leia hasn't always been that way. *What does she have to be afraid of?* you wonder.

You flash back to the man who grabbed you at the Oiled Gull last night. What did he say? "You surfers better stay out of our way, or we'll get more of you."

Adding this to what Joe said, you wonder if this is what Leia was afraid of—and if it has something to do with Jorge's disappearance. Maybe you should pay a visit to the Oiled Gull. It doesn't seem like a pleasant place, but you might find new evidence there about Jorge.

On the other hand, you feel a lot more at home at the cove. Perhaps you should go back to a familiar, peaceful place to puzzle things out. It might give you new inspiration.

*If you head down to the cove, turn to page 25.*

*If you go over to the Oiled Gull,
turn to page 94.*

Now you paddle back to shore, full of concern for Jorge. In spite of the teeth marks on his board, a shark attack leaving no trace of your friend seems unlikely. You have a feeling there's more to the situation than appears on the surface. As you tow Jorge's board and your own ashore, you decide to search for him, if only to put your mind at rest.

You start by scouring Jorge's favorite hangouts around the cove—the surfer's altar set in a cave high on the bluff, the abandoned hulk of an old Greek freighter at Shipwreck Point, and the steps around the lighthouse. But there's no sign of Jorge.

You lash both surfboards to your bike and ride into town to the surf shop. A hard-core group of surfers who call themselves the "Surf Monkeys" hangs out there. You're usually happy to keep your distance from them, but now you've got to find out if they have any clues about Jorge. Lately he seemed to be getting friendly with them, though he was a bit secretive about it.

Leia, the leader, is leaning on the shop counter, along with her buddies Lance, Bethany, and Tommy, when you enter. They don't bother to acknowledge you. You have to push into the center of the group with Jorge's damaged board before they'll even pay attention to your questions.

*Turn to page 6.*

"I've warned the oil company," Joe continues, "but they just don't listen. Their main interest is in making money, and they don't really care what happens to the ocean in the process. They say their rig can withstand a major earthquake. But I doubt it."

You follow Earthquake Joe back to his house. As you approach, a German shepherd slinks outside, whimpering. It comes over to lean, trembling, against its master. "It's okay, Ben," Joe says, trying to comfort the dog.

Joe invites you into his tiny house. It's filled with cages of birds and mice, and tanks of fish, frogs, and turtles. You glance out the window and notice the yard is also full of animals—goats, roosters, and an old mule who is pawing the ground, its ears pricked.

"These guys are my earthquake predictors," Earthquake Joe explains. He then leads you into the bathroom. The bathtub is taken up with a giant old seismograph. Hundreds of tiny arms graph lines across a slowly turning drum.

"There were a few small tremors last night," Joe says, pointing out some jags in the lines.

"I thought I didn't sleep very well," you comment.

Then you remember the reason you came into the hills in the first place. "This is all very interesting," you say to Joe, "but actually I was wondering if you knew anything about a friend of mine who's been missing for a few days."

*Turn to page 104.*

"Yeah, I've been out a couple of times to take a look," Leia says.

"How did Jorge end up on the rig?" you ask.

"Shhhhh," says Leia. You pause, puzzled, before you realize that Leia is listening to the foghorns to get a read on her position. She stops and sits up abruptly, peering hard into the fog. "Oh no," she says in a low voice. "Say your prayers." Then she shouts so everyone can hear, "Get out of here—fast!"

You look up and see a dark shape looming high above you in the fog—it's the tanker, bearing down on you at full speed!

There's no way the tanker captain will see you, and even if he did, it would take a ship that size at least a mile to stop. You and the other Surf Monkeys paddle furiously. Your heart pounds as you frantically pull at the dark water. A deafening blast comes from the horn of the ship. It sounds as if the tanker is almost on top of you. A blind panic takes over your body.

All at once a swell lifts the back of your board. It's the wake coming off the tanker's prow, you realize. Your only chance is to surf the wake clear of the giant ship. With a couple of swift paddles, you manage to jump to your feet and aim the board straight down the face of the big wake.

*Turn to page 56.*

# 78

You're about to leave when the pub's owner, Mo, beckons you over to the end of the counter. You're sure you're going to get thrown out, but you walk over to her anyway. She has a weathered face and clear green eyes and is wearing an apron over her clothes.

"Can I help you?" she asks, wiping a glass. Surprised by Mo's friendliness, you show her the picture of Jorge. Just then the glasses hanging over the counter begin to clink against each other, and you feel the floor shifting strangely under you. Mo looks at you and says, "Did you feel that?"

You're about to reply when a strong jolt throws you backward off the barstool onto the floor. You look up to see the room swaying above you. Everyone is scrambling for the door. You're not sure what's happening.

The next thing you know, Mo is helping you to your feet. "Quick, get in the doorway," she says. "It's an earthquake!"

*Of course! Joe was right*, you realize as you cram into the doorway along with everybody else. Outside you can see telephone poles swaying wildly and glass bursting from windows. Behind you the tables are walking furiously around the room, and the chairs are falling over backward as if full of rest-less ghosts. Giant cracks open up in the ceiling. There's nothing you can do but hang on.

*Turn to page 53.*

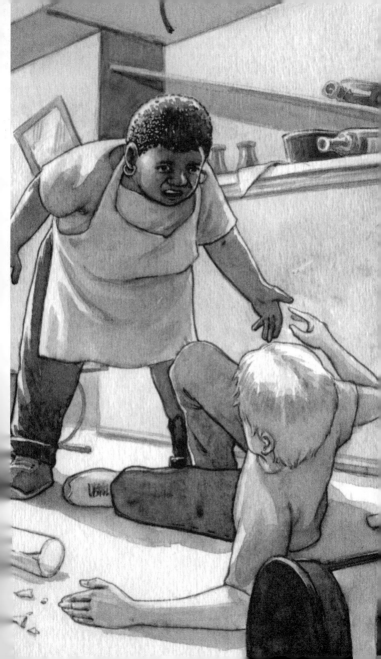

You hadn't planned on the rig workers being so hostile—or armed. Now you realize with a shock that they're deadly serious about getting rid of you and Jorge.

"You'll never get away with this," you say. But your words lack conviction. Annie grabs you roughly and drags you in the direction of the gangplank. When you try to resist, she raises her arm. You feel a sharp pain in the center of your forehead, and everything goes black.

You wake to a low rumble and the thick smell of oil. Your hands and feet are bound. Wherever you are, it is extremely cold and dark. As your eyes adjust, you can make out Jorge lying beside you. You lean closer. He's breathing but unconscious.

You struggle to your knees and peer through a porthole. Far below, you can see the deep blue chop of open ocean. Then it comes back to you. You must be in the hull of the supertanker, headed to Alaska. Involuntarily, you start to shiver.

Well, at least you found Jorge. And who knows, maybe the surfing will be great in Alaska. But you really wish you'd brought along your booties.

**The End**

Joe shrugs. "I'm done worrying about it. People don't want to listen to a crazy old guy living in the hills. They just want to keep on buying their cheap gasoline, driving to the malls—and looking out and seeing all that safe, cheap energy being pumped out of the bottom of the ocean." You glance up at Joe and watch a grim smile cross his face as he adds, "Not."

You nod wearily. You have to admit you wouldn't pay any attention to Joe, either, if you hadn't been drawn into this whole mystery through Jorge. You push yourself out of the armchair with a grunt and say, "Well, I'd better get moving."

Joe sticks out his hand and says, "Glad to have met you. Good luck finding your friend." You thank Joe for his hospitality. "Stay away from tall buildings and power lines today," he calls after you as you ride off.

*Turn to page 74.*

As you wriggle out of the man's grasp, he snarls after you, "You surfers better stay out of our way, or we'll get more of you." Then he reels off in the direction of the harbor, leaving behind the reek of diesel.

You have no idea what to make of the man's threat. *Could it have something to do with Jorge's disappearance?* you wonder.

*Go on to the next page.*

You're too tired to puzzle it out now. Wearily, you put the incident out of your mind and trudge back to your uncle's house. When you finally make it home, you notice greasy black fingerprints on your jacket where the man grabbed you. *He must have been one of the guys working on the oil rig,* you think.

You awaken late the next morning. Groggily you recall last night and the exhilaration of shooting the pier. But then your spirits fall as you remember your original reason for joining the Surf Monkeys. You're no closer to solving the puzzle of Jorge's disappearance than you were this time yesterday morning.

A note is tacked to the refrigerator in the kitchen. *Gone fishing. Big salmon run up the coast—back in three days. Take care, Uncle Dave.*

*That's okay,* you think. You'll be able to keep looking for Jorge without having to explain yourself.

*Turn to page 24.*

# 86

Diving through the surf on the dolphin's back, you begin to feel that you and the animal are one. You have an overwhelming sense of belonging that seems to come from the dolphin itself. It's easy to imagine that all forms of life—including yourself—originated in the bright, salty waves. *Maybe it was a mistake to drag ourselves up on dry land*, you think.

A dark shadow brings you out of your reveries. It's as if the sun has been eclipsed. You look up in shock to see the giant oil rig looming above you. The dolphin slows down as you approach a small dock. You slide off its back and swim for the dock, thinking, *I'm obviously getting dropped off here.*

Another dolphin swims forward, carrying the surf leash on its snout. You reach down from the dock to grab it. The dolphin dives, and you say, "So this is where you think Jorge is, huh? I hope you're right."

From below you can't see anyone on the rig. It's Sunday, you remember. All the rig workers are probably ashore, which means this is a good chance for you to look around. You turn back to the dolphins, who are still watching you from the water.

"Stay here," you say. "I'll need a ride back." You only hope they'll understand.

*Turn to page 31.*

*Dolphins!* you realize with great relief. Turning, you find that you're surrounded by a pod of the beautiful gray and white creatures. They seem to be playing ring-around-the-rosy, with you in the middle. You're close enough to see the intelligent sparkle in their eyes as they lift their heads out of the water.

Then you notice that the dolphins are playing with some kind of line, passing it back and forth with their long snouts.

"I can play that game, too," you say, trying to grab the line. When you see it up close, you realize it's a surfboard leash. And you recognize the ankle strap: red, with black Velcro—just like Jorge's!

You also notice that the leash is covered with tar. As you look at the dolphins, you wish you could speak their high-pitched, echoing language so you could ask them where they got the leash. You try making a few squeaks anyway, imitating the dolphins.

*Turn to page 100.*

"But when we got out there the other night, we discovered they'd put armed guards on the rig," Jorge continues. "The others got away, but I was caught. The rig workers kept me prisoner on the rig, trying to decide what to do with me. I was sure I was never going to see anyone ever again after they told me I was going to Alaska."

"Me, either," you say. You recount how you found his surfboard with its shark-teeth marks. "I really thought you'd been eaten alive until I saw the S.O.S. scratched in the wax. Suddenly there seem to be lots of sharks around."

"I can explain that," Jorge says. "See, the rig workers decided that sharks were the best way to keep us surfers out of the water. So they set up a shark cage down below the oil rig. They catch sharks and keep them in there, without feeding them for weeks. When the sharks are good and hungry, they let them go. Naturally, the sharks head for shore and bite at anything—even surfers."

By now the Surf Monkeys are listening, the rig workers securely tied up. Leia shakes her head in disgust.

You're shocked the rig workers could be so cruel. "Every surfer in the water will be attacked!" you say incredulously. "Something's got to be done."

"Yeah, but not now. I haven't slept in three days," Jorge moans.

*Turn to page 8.*

You bravely climb into a rusty green car. Almost instantly it lurches forward with a horrible screech. Slowly it begins to grind up the first incline. Your heart is pounding as you come closer and closer to the top of the giant hill.

The car crests the hill. For a moment, everything seems to stand still. You look down to see the Surf Monkeys far below, looking up at you. The lights of the town stretch out behind you, and in front is the dark, deserted ocean.

The rickety cars plunge. They shake violently in their screaming descent, reach the bottom with a bone-crushing jolt, then race up the next hill. But as you crest the top of the roller coaster's highest point, there is a tearing sound. Suddenly the screeching and shaking stop. There is nothing but silence.

With horror you realize you're no longer attached to the track—you're airborne, heading straight out over the beach toward the dark ocean. As the wind whistles past your ears, your only hope is that the waves are good in surfer heaven.

**The End**

You slip down to a supply room you passed on the way and grab a pair of giant bolt cutters, which you take back to apply to Jorge's chains.

"We've got to get off this rig, and fast," Jorge says. "I overheard some guy on a shortwave radio last night say there's going to be an earthquake soon."

"That was Earthquake Joe!" you exclaim.

"I don't care if it was the President of the United States, I just don't want to be on this rig when it hits."

"What are you doing out here in the first place?" you snap.

"Uh, well," Jorge says, suddenly at a loss. "I was doing Leia a favor. The Surf Monkeys were trying to stop the construction of the rig. They thought it was too dangerous, and an oil spill would ruin the surfing. They tried to talk to the oil company, but no one would listen. Then they started coming out to the rig at night and messing things up—wrecking the equipment and throwing machinery over the side. They recruited me because they needed someone small enough to get into the drilling rig and steal the drill bit. We all paddled out together, but when we got here that night there were armed guards on the rig. I got nabbed. The rest of them got away and never came back for me."

"That explains all the equipment I found in the lighthouse—the diving suits, blowtorches, and monkey wrenches," you say.

*Turn to page 49.*

You pedal down to the Oiled Gull as fast as you can. You're nervous as you approach the swinging doors, the roar of a televised preseason football game and frenzied shouts coming from inside. A sign tacked next to the door reads: NO ONE UNDER 21 ALLOWED. NO BARE FEET.

*Well, one out of two's not bad*, you think, taking a deep breath and pushing through the doors. The place is full of rig workers, most of whom are shoveling down big plates of eggs and potatoes for breakfast. But a few have already bellied up to the counter, even though it's before noon, their faces lit by the blue glow of the television.

No one looks up when you come in. You search the tables, but there's no sign of the man who grabbed you last night. You're not sure what to do. Then you remember the picture of Jorge that's still in your pocket. You pull yourself up on an empty stool and turn to the man sitting next to you.

"Excuse me," you say, holding up the picture. "I wonder if you've seen a friend of mine around here."

The man looks at you, glances at the picture, then shakes his head and goes back to watching the game. You show the picture to several more people and get the same response.

*Turn to page 78.*

You catch a few hours of sleep on the couch, then go down to the police station first thing in the morning. You're shown to the office of a big bulldog of a sergeant who glowers at you from underneath a buzzcut.

"I'm a busy man," he says. "You better not be wasting my time."

"No sir," you promise. "My friend Jorge is being held prisoner on the *Alpha Yankee* oil rig. You've got to rescue him."

The sergeant leans forward.

"What was this guy Jorge doing out on the rig? Is he a surfer?"

The gruff question takes you by surprise. "Well, yeah…"

"I thought so," the sergeant says, his eyes boring into you. "You surfers have been out there causing trouble on that rig ever since they started building it. What do they call it?" He thinks for a minute, then pronounces the words with distaste. "Monkey wrenching. Is that what your buddy was doing?"

"No, I'm sure he wasn't," you reply in a quavering voice. You begin backing out of the room, deciding you better cut out before the sergeant thinks of detaining you for questioning. "Uh, well, thanks anyway," you say. The sergeant's face remains impassive as you give some sort of salute, turn, and leave the station as fast as you can.

*Turn to the next page.*

*Now what?* you think. Obviously the police aren't going to help. And you can't just wander around aimlessly all day, hoping that Jorge will somehow magically appear.

Later that night, you get an idea. You grab your skateboard and head down to the harbor at the north end of the bay. There you find the harbor patrol office, a rickety structure at the top of a flight of stairs. Inside, you see the night harbor master leaning back in his chair—fast asleep.

*Turn to page 118.*

You take a deep breath, then dive from the top story of the rig into the ocean.

You don't know if the dolphins were waiting for you, but they leap into the air when they see you diving off the rig. Then they dive underwater to bring you back to the surface. You and Jorge each grab a dolphin, and they start to head for shore. You look back to see the guard on the rig staring down at you in stunned amazement.

When you near land, the dolphins suddenly stop. They float still in the water, as if listening. Suddenly you see the houses along the beach moving in a wave. Then a giant wall of water appears behind you. You and Jorge wrap your arms tightly around the dolphins as they dive underwater with you until the monster wave has passed.

*Turn to page 124.*

One of the dolphins swims up to you and nudges your hand with its snout. It turns and swims up against you again, then stays still in the water. You hesitate, and it dives beneath you, swimming playfully between your legs. It comes to you again, prodding you with its dorsal fin.

"You want to take me for a ride?" you ask. "Well, why not?"

You gently take hold of the dolphin's soft gray fin and straddle its back. A thrill goes through you as its strong, taut body pulls you through the surf. The dolphin picks up speed, and the rest of the pod dives alongside. It takes all your might to hold onto the dolphin's slippery fin as it plunges up and down in the rough water.

It's an incredible sensation to be flying through the surf. You're having so much fun that you haven't noticed where you're going. Looking up, you see the dolphin is taking you straight out to sea!

You keep hold of the dolphin's fin, trusting your strong sense that they're trying to help you. You know dolphins are extremely intelligent. When they look at you with their gray, humanlike eyes, you almost feel that they know what you're thinking.

*Turn to page 86.*

But no one would listen to them. So finally they decided to take things into their own hands and "monkey wrench" the rig. They would come out to the rig at night and throw pieces of machinery into the ocean to delay construction. But when that failed to stop the rig, they decided to take more extreme measures.

"That's when they recruited me," Jorge explains. "The Surf Monkeys needed someone to climb into the drilling mechanism and detach the diamond-tipped drilling bit. It's a very expensive part, and it would take months to replace. I was the only one small enough for the job.

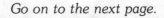

*Go on to the next page.*

"We came out three nights ago. But when we arrived, the rig was guarded by armed workers—hired thugs. They nabbed me trying to get into the drilling mechanism, but the rest of the Surf Monkeys got away. The thugs waited for Mai, their ringleader, to come back and decide what to do with me. Meanwhile, they put me to work during the day doing the dirtiest jobs on the rig. At night, they kept me chained to a crane.

"They got the rig started yesterday. It's pumping oil up from the ocean floor right now. I managed to get my hands on a shaving mirror and flashlight, which I used to signal the shore every night after the workers went home. But I guess no one saw my S.O.S."

*Turn to page 52.*

You pull out the picture of Jorge to show Joe.

"I've never seen your friend," Earthquake Joe says. "But I know a surfer named Leia. She was a real sincere kid. She used to come up and visit me. She was concerned about that oil rig and the danger of spills. She wanted me to talk to the oil company about it. But the oil executives refused to meet with us and wouldn't return our phone calls. Leia got mad and said something about taking direct action. I hope she didn't get into any trouble. I myself believe in nonviolence."

Is Earthquake Joe talking about the same Leia you know? Sincere is the last word you'd use to describe Leia. Yet Joe seems to respect her.

You plop down in a dusty old armchair in Joe's living room. The more you hear, the worse it gets. All of a sudden you feel overwhelmed by it all. Jorge has been missing for four days now, and you're not any closer to finding him. Leia, who you have reason to believe betrayed your friend, turns out to be a buddy of Earthquake Joe's. And an earthquake is going to destroy the oil rig, causing untold destruction up and down the coast, particularly to the cove.

"What's the matter?" Joe asks. "Why so glum?"

*Go on to the next page.*

"I don't know," you say with a heavy sigh. "I just wish I could figure out what the connection is between Jorge, Leia, and the oil rig."

"Hmmmm," Joe says, stroking his beard. "Too bad I don't have a system that can figure that one out."

You cock your head. "Joe, how can you just sit here, knowing there's going to be a disastrous earthquake soon?"

*Turn to page 82.*

"Forget it, Leia," you say, pushing the throttle to full and heading the boat for shore. "We've had enough excitement for one night."

Leia looks to the rest of her gang but doesn't find the support she needs. "Okay, gremmie. But if an earthquake hits tomorrow, you're dog meat."

"I'll take full responsibility," you say sarcastically.

You're relieved to finally get back to shore. You tie up the boat, and leave the tied-up rig workers at the dock. Wearily you shake hands with the Surf Monkeys, then head back with Jorge to your uncle's house for some well-deserved rest.

That morning you're pried out of a heavy sleep by a violent shaking. It takes you a while to come to, and when you finally do, the shaking has stopped. You're not sure what caused it, but you decide to get dressed and find out.

Jorge has snoozed right through the ruckus. You leave him sleeping on the couch and head outside. All kinds of people are gathered on the street. You listen long enough to find that what they're all talking about is "the earthquake."

So that's what it was. A creeping sense of dread overcomes you as you proceed toward the beachfront. Already you can see a plume of thick black smoke rising into the sky offshore. You find people gathered at the water, too, watching the oil rig burn. Someone points out a gob of black liquid spreading from the burning rig across the water.

*Turn to page 120.*

"The Surf Monkeys are too much trouble," you mutter to yourself on your way home to Uncle Dave's house. You'll keep looking for Jorge on your own, you decide.

Dave isn't home when you get there, so you flop down on the couch. Soon you're fast asleep. You wake to the sound of the front door opening as Dave returns. It's dark outside.

"Guess what!" Dave exclaims. "There's a monster salmon run up the coast. I'm leaving tonight—want to come?"

"I can't," you say, rubbing your eyes. "Jorge has disappeared, and I've got to find him." You go on to explain what's happened since the day before yesterday.

"Hmmmm," Dave says, pulling at his goatee. His eyes wander toward an old ship-to-shore radio collecting dust on his desk. He motions you over, and together you click it on and start to play with the dials. All you get is static for a while, then some Vietnamese fishermen.

"I've got to get geared up for my fishing expedition," Dave says, leaving you to the radio.

You still haven't found anything interesting by the time Dave is packing his jeep. He asks one last time if you don't want to come with him. "I can't leave Jorge behind," you explain.

"Okay, but listen," Dave says. "If he doesn't turn up by tomorrow morning, you've got to go to the police. It doesn't matter who he is—if he's met up with foul play, you need the police."

*Turn to page 16.*

Both of you know what you have to do. With a running start, you and Jorge leap over the edge of the railing and plunge to the madly churning water below. After struggling to the surface, you swim to the anchor chain where you left your paddleboard. You glance over at the dock, which is tossing wildly. You're surprised to see the launch gone, and Mai and Annie with it—they must have gotten it turned over. But right now, it's your own escape you're worried about.

Somehow you and Jorge manage to untie your paddleboard from the anchor chain. You climb on, and Jorge gets on behind you. You both paddle madly as the first huge swell reaches you. You've never ridden a wave this big before—it's like paddling down the side of a mountain.

As the momentum of the swell begins to propel you forward, you and Jorge both get up on the board, crouching, your knees bent in an attempt to control it.

"We got it!" Jorge shouts in your ear over the deafening roar of the wave.

The swell grows larger and steeper as it moves toward the shore. You're still a mile out when the wave begins to curl.

"It's starting to break!" you cry to Jorge.

He just nods and bears down on the board with you. The tip of the giant wave arcs high over your heads. Suddenly you and Jorge are completely enclosed in a giant green tube, roaring toward the beach at incredible speed.

*Turn to page 66.*

# 110

You summon all the bravado you can and say, "Let's shoot the pier." At least this way, you reason, your fate will be determined by your surfing talent, not the condition of some rusty roller coaster.

The Surf Monkeys give a whoop. You all jump up, grab your boards, and head down toward the beach. Soon the pounding of giant surf on the dark beach is thundering in your ears. You have a sick feeling in your stomach. You've only shot the pier once—and you've never surfed at night.

You grip your board and plunge into the black water with the others, guiding yourself out by sheer instinct. When you reach the lineup, where the surfers each wait in turn to catch a ride, you can hear the dull thud of waves hitting the pier pilings. The Surf Monkeys take off one by one on the huge swells, disappearing with screams into the darkness.

Only you and Leia remain. You know the rest are waiting for you on the other side of the pier. During a lull in the roar, you think you detect a note of sympathy in her voice as Leia says, "It's your turn, gremmie."

A swell approaches. As you paddle out to catch it, you notice for the first time that the water has a luminous glow. You plunge your hands in and stir up a luminescent red eddy. *A red tide!* you think— the glow caused by an influx of phosphorescent plankton. It could be your salvation, since the water churning around the pier pilings will be glowing, too.

*Turn to page 20.*

Suddenly you're wide awake, unable to believe what you just heard. The surfer they're talking about has to be Jorge. He disappeared last night. And now he's being shipped to Alaska!

You stand frozen in the middle of the living room, feeling completely helpless. When did the *Polar Bear* say they were going to sail? Zero three two niner. That's 3:29 a.m. tomorrow.

You've got to find a way to get to Jorge before then—but how? Suddenly you wish Uncle Dave were still here. Your next thought is of the Surf Monkeys—surely they'd want to help rescue Jorge, if you could get them to listen to you long enough to explain the situation.

On the other hand, maybe they wouldn't. You have a nagging suspicion they might be the ones who got Jorge in trouble in the first place. They might just deny everything. Maybe you'd better go to the police, as Dave suggested, although you don't even know Jorge's last name.

*If you decide to ask the Surf Monkeys for help, turn to page 44.*

*If you think you should go to the police, turn to page 95.*

# 112

You're startled by the long, low blast of a ship's horn. You look back to see a giant supertanker passing close by, headed out to sea.

"You're just in time for an all-expense-paid trip to Alaska," the scar-faced man is saying to Jorge. "How does a little arctic surfing sound?" You can tell from his tone of voice that he's serious.

"You got the launch ready, Mai?" the woman asks him.

"'Course it's ready, Annie," Mai answers. "What do you think—I've been relaxing all night?"

The woman chuckles. You hear a thud and a gasp as Mai knees Jorge and says, "Get over there, surfer. Your cruise ship awaits."

You size up the situation quickly. From what you can tell, they intend to take Jorge down to the small launch waiting at the dock below, and from there to the passing supertanker—which is on its way to Alaska.

Things are happening too quickly. Is this the time to make your move? You could step out and try to free Jorge now, but you're not sure how much of a chance you have against the two workers. Should you wait for a less risky opening?

Unfortunately, there's only one way to find out.

---

*If you stay in your hiding place and wait for another opening, turn to page 14.*

*If you jump out and try to free Jorge, turn to page 55.*

"You don't understand," Leia says. "This isn't just about Jorge. It's turf. They're trying to intimidate us, and we've got to show them it won't work. If we let them get away with this, they'll think they've won the battle for the ocean."

Leia pauses and fixes the group with her piercing eyes. "I, for one, am not ready to give up yet. I'm not saying it'll be easy, but I'm going out there tonight. Who's with me?"

The Surf Monkeys glance at each other. All but Lance give a nod.

"All right," Leia says in a calm voice. "Meet back here at midnight. We've got a mission."

*Turn to page 65.*

Then you see what looks like the dark head of a seal, swimming toward you through the billowing smoke and flames. You shove the throttle forward and head over to it as fast as you can. As you get closer, you realize it's not a seal, but a person, covered with a thick, black coat of oil. *He must have jumped from the rig before it blew*, you think.

You pull up alongside the figure, your heart pounding. Leaning over, you manage to pull the half-conscious swimmer into the boat. You take off your jacket and start to wipe the oil off the swimmer's face. Only then do you realize, to your astonishment, that it's Jorge!

"I can't believe it's you—you made it!" you exclaim.

Jorge lies in the prow of the boat, gasping for breath. "Me neither, man," he replies. "I thought monkey wrenching was a joke. Boy, was I wrong. Those thugs they hired to guard the rig are the nastiest I've ever met. They tried to put me on a tanker headed for Alaska!"

Jorge pauses and shakes his head. "Not my idea of summer vacation."

You turn the boat and head back to shore. Later, Jorge tries to run his hand through the sticky mass of petroleum in his hair. "I'll tell you what else," he adds, the old wicked grin returning to his face. "This is the first and last time I grease back my hair."

**The End**

The next morning you unroll the map to get a better look. It shows the mountains behind town. Someone's marked a trail on it that ends in an X. *Is this another Surf Monkey hideout*, you wonder— *or possibly even where Jorge is?* You'll have to follow the map and see where it leads you.

You borrow your uncle's mountain bike for the ride into the hills. A trailhead that seems to match the one on the map leads straight up into a steep canyon of redwoods. At the head of the canyon a sign says RESEARCH AREA: KEEP OUT. You ignore the sign. After all, you figure what you're doing could be considered research.

You walk along a small stream for a while, trying to keep track of the trail. All of a sudden you come upon a gray-bearded man gazing down into a small green pond.

Bubbles rise to the surface of the pond. Then, to your amazement, a spurt of water shoots straight up into the air.

"I knew it!" the man shouts, jumping up and down in front of the pool. "Oh, it's going to be a big one!"

"A big what?" you ask. The man turns, startled at the sound of your voice.

"An earthquake!" he shouts. "The pressure on this fault is so extreme right now that it's making water shoot up out of the ground. Look at this."

He leads you into an open grassy field. Something brushes your foot. Hundreds of snakes are squiggling through the grass!

*Turn to page 5.*

# 118

You rap on the harbor master's glass door and shout, without result. Then you notice the schedule on the door. He's off duty and sound asleep. He'd be so grumpy if you woke him up that he wouldn't be much help.

You go back down the stairs, looking over the harbor. It's quiet except for a few Vietnamese fishermen warming up their engines and working on their nets before going out on their nightly fishing expeditions. One boat has candles and incense burning on a small altar in the bow. The fishermen are kneeling in front of the altar, intoning a deep-voiced Buddhist chant.

One more possibility occurs to you. Maybe your uncle's fishing boat is within radio hailing distance. You approach one of the fishermen and convince him to let you use his ship-to-shore radio.

*Go on to the next page.*

"This is an urgent call for the *Cowabunga*. Uncle Dave, are you out there? Over."

All you get is static. You try several times but have no luck. You're just putting the transmitter down when you hear the long, low blast of a freighter's horn. You run up on deck just in time to see a supertanker heading out to sea. You can just make out its name—the *Polar Bear*, just as you feared. Two tugboats are dropping the lines and backing away. The enormous black-hulled tanker, riding high in the water, is soon enveloped in thick fog.

*Jorge's going to have a long trip*, you think helplessly. You may never find out how he ended up on the tanker. And you have a horrible feeling you may never see him again, either.

**The End**

Soon the cove, and the entire coast, will be blanketed in oil. With a sick feeling in your stomach you turn and scurry back to your uncle's. Leia's words from the night before run through your mind. *It's time to pack my bags*, you think, *and get myself back home to Indiana.*

## The End

You get back home and collapse, exhausted from being up since five in the morning. When you wake it's already dark. You go out into the yard and look once more at Jorge's board. Unfortunately, it wasn't a dream. Jorge is either dead, wounded, or playing a nasty trick on you.

The moon is just coming up over the hills. In its angled beams you notice something you hadn't seen before—scratched deeply into the wax on the deck of the board are the letters "S.O.S."!

You resume your search first thing the next morning. You start at the police station, but they have no news of anyone matching Jorge's description. You're not sure what Jorge's last name is, and you know he's living here without his parents, so you decide against filing a missing person report.

You go down to the beach to talk to the life-guards. They act doubtful when you ask about a shark attack. They tell you there hasn't been a shark attack that close to shore in twenty years. Only divers in much deeper water have been attacked.

That afternoon you head out with your board to Shipwreck Point, a Surf Monkey hangout. Years ago a Greek freighter ran aground in a thick fog. The ship broke in half, and now its rusty bow juts up out of the water. The rest of the ship is strewn across the rocks.

*Turn to page 11.*

Jorge is gagged and blindfolded, and his hands and feet are wrapped in chains. "It's me," you pant. "How are you doing, buddy?"

Jorge gives a shrug of his shoulders and moans through the gag. You set to work loosening the chains enough for him to wriggle his hands out of them. Then he works the gag and blindfold off while you get the chains on his feet loosened.

"Hey, you okay?" you ask, gripping Jorge by both shoulders.

"Yeah, I think so. Where are we? How'd you find me?" He glances over at Leia and the other Surf Monkeys in the back of the boat, who are still dealing with the two people.

"I'll explain in a minute," you say, moving to the driver's seat of the motorboat. "First tell me how you got out here—and how you got to be so buddy-buddy with Leia."

Jorge hangs his head a little and says, "I became a Surf Monkey." He jerks his thumb in the direction of the oil rig. "It's all because of that thing. Leia convinced me that it was too dangerous to have a rig pumping out oil right alongside a fault line—which is what it's built on. Once I joined up, Leia said she had a special mission for me.

*Go on to the next page.*

"The Surf Monkeys had been going out at night and messing with the rig's equipment to try to delay the building. But once it was finished, they needed to take more drastic action. If they could get hold of the drill bit, they could delay the pumping of oil by several weeks. I was the only one small enough to climb into the drill shaft itself and detach the bit."

*Turn to page 88.*

By the time the dolphins bring you back to the surface, you're gasping for breath. "Did you see those houses lifting up?" Jorge says. "That must have been the earthquake!"

"The one Joe predicted," you add.

Then Jorge's eyes grow wide. You follow his gaze to see that the giant oil rig has collapsed onto its side and is rapidly sinking.

The dolphins take a few leaps into the air, then head with you toward the beach. Jorge seems lost in thought. Finally he looks over at you and asks, "How'd you get to be so friendly with these dolphins, anyway?"

"I guess we just speak the same language," you reply, figuring it will take Jorge a while at least to puzzle that one out.

**The End**

# ABOUT THE ARTISTS

**Illustrator: Gabhor Utomo** was born in Indonesia. He moved to California to pursue his passion in art. He received his degree from Academy of Art University in San Francisco in spring 2003. Since his graduation he has worked as a freelance illustrator and has illustrated a number of children's books. Gabhor lives with his wife, Dina, and his twin girls in the San Francisco Bay Area.

**Cover Illustrator: Marco Cannella** was born in Ascoli Piceno, Italy, on September 29, 1972. Marco started his career in art as a decorator and an illustrator when he was a college student. He became a full-time professional in 2001 when he received the flag-prize for the "Palio della Quintana" (one of the most important Italian historical games). Since then, he has worked as an illustrator at Studio Inventario in Bologna. He has also been a scenery designer for professional theater companies. He works for the production company ASP srl in Rome as a character designer and set designer on the preproduction of a CG feature film. In 2004 he moved to Bangalore, India, to serve as full-time art director on this project.

# ABOUT THE AUTHOR

**JAY LEIBOLD** was born in Denver, Colorado. Jay has written *Secret of the Ninja*, *Sabotage*, *Grand Canyon Odyssey*, *Spy For George Washington*, *Return of the Ninja*, *The Search for Aladdin's Lamp*, *You are a Millionaire*, *Beyond the Great Wall*, *Revenge of the Russian Ghost*, *Surf Monkeys*, and *Ninja Cyborg* in the *Choose Your Own Adventure®* series.

**For games, activities, and other fun stuff, or to write to Chooseco, visit us online at CYOA.com**

# JOURNEY
## UNDER THE SEA

CHOOSE
FROM 42
ENDINGS

BY R. A. MONTGOMERY

CHOOSE YOUR OWN ADVENTURE® 6
HOUSE OF DANGER
CHOOSE FROM 20 ENDINGS!
BY R. A. MONTGOMERY

# ESCAPE

CHOOSE
FROM **27**
ENDINGS

**BY R. A. MONTGOMERY**